THE EXTRAORDINARY A

MR BENN

SPACEMAN

Based on the TV series by David McKee

Hodder
Children's
Books

A division of Hodder Children's Books

Spaceman
First published in 1993
This edition published in 2013

Text copyright © David Mckee 1993
Illustrations copyright © King Rollo Films Ltd 1993

Hodder Children's Books, 338 Euston Road, London, NW1 3BH
Hodder Children's Books Australia, Level 17/207 Kent Street, Sydney, NSW 2000

The rights of David McKee to be identified as the author of the text of this work and of
King Rollo Films Ltd to be identified as the illustrator of this work have been asserted
by them in accordance with the Copyright, Designs and Patent Act 1988.

ISBN: 978 1 909 76803 1

Printed in China

Hodder Children's Books is a division of Hachette Children's Books.
An Hachette UK Company.

www.hachette.co.uk

It was just an ordinary day in Festive Road.
Boys played with toy rockets while their mothers
brought home the shopping.

Number 52 was Mr Benn's house but he was
nowhere to be seen.

Mr Benn was in the back garden talking to his neighbour.

"Why is it," asked the neighbour, "that your grass looks greener than mine?"

"That's strange," said Mr Benn, "I always think yours looks greener than mine." And they both laughed.

Mr Benn decided to go for a walk in the park.
He sat on a bench and watched a boy flying a kite.

"I wonder if it would go above the clouds if the string
was long enough," he thought. "It would be so
interesting to go up above the clouds."

All of a sudden Mr Benn tingled with excitement
as he remembered the costume shop.

In almost no time at all, Mr Benn was in the special shop where adventures start. As if by magic, the shopkeeper appeared.

"Good morning, sir. I do believe you've made up your mind already."

"I'd like to try the space outfit," said Mr Benn.

"You know the way, sir," replied the shopkeeper, pointing to the changing room.

Mr Benn changed into the space outfit. He looked at himself in the mirror and then headed for the door that always led to adventures.

On the other side he found himself in a spaceship.
Another spaceman was at the controls.

"Hello," he said, "ready for the blast off? Here we go then."

Mr Benn felt the spaceship surge as it lifted off.

"Where are we going?" said Mr Benn as he watched the stars through the window.

"To a planet covered with gold and jewels. We'll be rich," said the spaceman.

"That would be fun," thought Mr Benn. But all he could see was a very ordinary planet.

The spaceship landed with a bump. Lying all around were lumps of glittering gold and jewels, just as the spaceman had said.

"We're rich!" said the spaceman. And they walked around picking up the best jewels and pieces of gold they could find.

All of a sudden they met a man dressed in rags, sitting on a lump of gold.

"Hello," said the man. "What are you going to do with that load?"

The spaceman laughed, "We're rich. We can do anything we like."

"I'm afraid you're wrong," said the ragged man. "It's no good to you at all. There are no shops on this planet so there's nowhere to spend the riches. Anyway, as soon as you leave this planet they turn into ordinary stones. The next planet is the place to be. There they live in comfort and everything is free."

"In that case, we may as well go to the next planet," said the spaceman. So they put down their gold and jewels and made their way back to the spaceship.

But Mr Benn took one piece of gold with him to see what it would look like when it changed to stone.

The spaceship zoomed away from the planet on its journey.

"There it is," said the spaceman, as they spotted another planet coming very close.

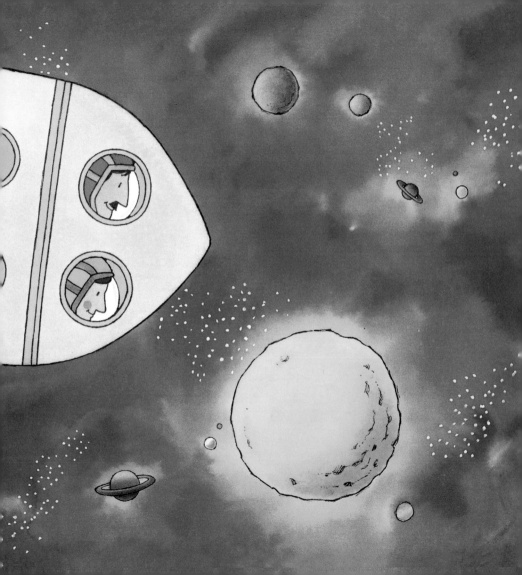

The spaceship landed near a town. Mr Benn and the spaceman saw that the shops were full of things, and nobody looked poor. At restaurants people sat outside and ate for free. Mr Benn and the spaceman sat down too. But something was wrong. They noticed that apart from themselves everything looked colourless.

"Tell us about this dullness," they said to the waiter.

"Well," he said, "there's no colour here at all, and if you stay here very long, you'll be just like us. But **there** is another planet not far away where everything is very **bright**."

"That's for us," said the spac**eman**. "**Let's** go there. I don't fancy a life without colour."

Back in the spaceship, Mr Benn watched the grey planet getting smaller and smaller as they headed towards the next planet.

"I hope the next planet will be more colourful," said Mr Benn as they flew nearer.

"We'll have a good look round first," replied the spaceman. "And we won't get out if we see anything wrong."

Once they had landed, they peered out of the windows. Everything looked all right. Colourful birds flew past. There were bright flowers and trees. They saw gaily coloured houses. People dressed in vivid clothes were walking about.

Mr Benn and the spaceman looked through the telescopes just to make sure. The only unusual thing they could see was the hats that everyone wore pulled down over their ears.

"Just the fashion," said the spaceman. "Let's go outside."

But they soon realised that the hats were not just fashion. Everyone had their ears covered for one very good reason: the air was filled with the most horrible screeching noises.

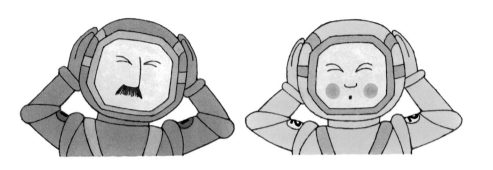

Mr Benn and the spaceman ran back to the spaceship and took off into the night. Before they had gone far, the spaceman said, "I'm lost. We'll have to stop at the next planet we pass and ask the way."

So once again they landed. This time the planet was very hot, too hot in fact, but at least it was quiet. Nobody was about. Then, as if by magic, a man appeared. It was the shopkeeper.

"We're lost," explained the spaceman. "We've been to all sorts of planets but we don't know where to go next."

"There is a place that is not altogether perfect, but then there is not much wrong with it either," said the shopkeeper.

"We'll try there," said the spaceman.

"I think I'll stay here," said Mr Benn. "I've had enough of travelling."

"It's very hot, sir," said the shopkeeper. "Step into the cave and keep cool."

Mr Benn went into the cave and, as he expected, he was back in the changing room of the shop. He changed into his own clothes.

"Where did you send the spaceman?" he asked as he returned the spaceman outfit.

"Here, sir, back to Earth," said the shopkeeper. "It's not perfect, but it's not too bad either."

Back in Festive Road, people went about their business as usual. At his gate, Mr Benn took the lump of stone out of his pocket.

"Nobody would believe that this was once gold," he thought. "But I'll always keep it. Then I will remember."